Charles Collins

The new year comes, my lady

Charles Collins

The new year comes, my lady

ISBN/EAN: 9783337118822

Printed in Europe, USA, Canada, Australia, Japan

Cover: Foto ©Andreas Hilbeck / pixelio.de

More available books at **www.hansebooks.com**

THE NEW YEAR COMES, MY LADY

BY

CHARLES H. COLLINS

AUTHOR OF "ECHOES FROM THE HIGHLAND HILLS,"
"FROM HIGHLAND HILLS TO AN EMPEROR'S TOMB," ETC.

BUFFALO
CHARLES WELLS MOULTON
1895

CONTENTS.

THE NEW YEAR
COMES, MY LADY

THE CAVERN BONES IN UTE PASS, COLORADO.

HOW long, oh tourist, did we wander, pray,
   In these dim aisles, the "long, long summer's
      day,"
Where silence awful, and the brooding night,
Appall the sense and strain the gazer's sight?
Deep under earth, the lantern fitful gleams,
On forms fantastic in this land of dreams,
Where the Great Architect of weal or woe,
Hath left unanswered, all we wish to know!
Whence came these sculptured spires, these shining
      cones,
This Gypsum dome--*this mass of crumbling bones?*

II.

What tales this cavern in the rugged peak
Could tell, if but these gloomy walls could speak!—
Who dared to enter *first* this dripping lair,
Of hanging bats, the emblem of despair?
Are these remains of savages or brutes,
Comanches, grizzlies, Navajoes or Utes,

9

Or pale-faced pilgrims on their weary march,
In search of gold at end of rainbow's arch,
Through the dread pass, who came in white array?
Where wait the Utes in ambush for their prey?

III.

Let fancy place behind each bush and stone,
The prowling Indian in cinctured zone,
And draw an image on the teeming brain,
Of sturdy trav'lers and the loaded wain,
Of prattling children and each faithful wife,
The shouldered rifles and the belted knife,
The dogs which 'neath the wagon jog along,
The pans and kettles with their jangling song.—
From shelving cliffs the sparkling streamlets flow,
To verdured parks which glimmer far below.

IV.

*   *   *   *   *   *

Midway the pass—the feathered arrows fly,
From crag and bush where secret foemen lie,
Entrapped, surrounded in the narrow glen,
'Tis but to fight—to die as fearless men,
Each rifle crack has stopped a demon's breath,
To yelling foes a messenger of death,
But all is vain! and o'er the blood-soaked vale,
At eve the circling vultures soaring sail.

And sneaking wolves scud from the distant plain
To whet their teeth in bodies of the slain.
Were the children killed?—see lying there
That row of little skulls—all scalped and bare.
While in Ute's retreat—in hills remote,
In wigwam smoke—their golden tresses float
Mid tufts of gray from grand sire's hoary head,
With fathers, mothers, numbered with the dead.

v.

The birds and wolves have cleaned each shining
      bone,
Ere darkness settles on her mountain throne.
The Utes and pilgrims who have met their doom,
Perhaps have found alike this caverned tomb
And here in heaps by torches' lurid glare,
We, stooping, ponder long "how came they
      there?"
To ONE alone the wherefore and the why
Of mysteries no mortal can descry,
The ONE who spoke in Sinai's thunder tones,
HE only knows *whence came, these crumbling
      bones?"*

VI.

The Utes are gone, their war whoops never more
Will echo through the glens where eagles soar,

No longer sounds on grassy park or dell
The wolf's long howl or Indian's curdling yell,
But Rainbow Falls still splash in tumbling spray,
Where summer tourists spend their holiday,
And through Ute Pass and down the cañon's side,
The laughing children on their burros ride,
Nor care for caverns with their dripping stones,
Their shapes grotesque or mass of crumbling
    bones.
For them the glad sunshine on the mountain's
    brow,
No need of the question, " *Where are we now ?* "
Since each cloud form castled with turrets high,
Each towering peak up reaching to the sky,
The myriad splendors of the earth and air,
Proclaim in glory " The Great Master's " care.

Manitou, Col., July, 1886.

WITH A SNOW FLOWER, NEW YEAR'S DAY. [1]

I.

TO thee, my friend, a simple flower
From Colorado snows,
Which bloomed in purple glory where
The tempest ever blows.
Oh, fair as the dream of early youth,
Or glimpse of rosy morn,
'Neath covering white in crumbling mold,
The little plant was born.

II.

'Tis withered now—a faded gem,
Too sweet, too rare, to last,
Away from its Rocky Mountain home,
A memory of the past.
A past of peaks, and giant forms,
Of blasted summits dead,
Where once 'mid rifts of gleaming snow,
It raised its modest head.

III.

Thus in the dreariest spots in life,
  The flowers of hope may spring,
To banish grief from earthly lot,
  A transient, flitting thing.
For every one climbs mountain heights,
  Each in our several way,
To find our visions of delight,
  Like snow flowers fade away.

IV.

And we will think of pleasant days,
  Although they come no more,
Of rainbows glowing in the skies,
  A glory as of yore.
Of sunbeams warm, in yellow light
  On all of earth below,
And flowers in dewy splendor born,
  'Mid Rocky Mountain snow.

January 1st, 1887.

ON PIKE'S PEAK.

I.

THE Falls are passed ; the trees are gone ;
   There lies the Gulch of Snow,
The circling eagles soaring sail
   In the depths far, far below !
The mist shapes form in gath'ring storm
   From out the frigid sky,
And wind-torn gorges, blasted rocks,
   Tumultuous 'round us lie.

II.

Through ermined clouds the light'ning's flash
   Glows in the purple west,
And rumbling thunders sullen roll
   Around the mountain's crest.
In chasms dense the shadows fall,
   And flitting sunbeams play,
Where trend the verdured eastern plains
   A hundred leagues away !

15

III.

On caverned cliffs, gemmed Manitou
　　A kerchief seems of lace,
A glimpse of white from borders green,
　　A smile upon her face.
And the red, red Garden of the Gods,
　　Fantastic to the sight,
With columns huge in distant glens,
　　Dwarfs its titanic might.

IV.

How puny all these giant domes,
　　How shrunk the foothills are,
Yon city but a simple dot,
　　So near—and yet so far !
The wreaths of fog have lifted up,
　　There is the signal mast !
The continent below us spreads,
　　This summit reached at last !

V.

Bring forth the emblem of our land,
　　Amidst the dashing hail,
The striped banner of the free,
　　Unfurl it to the gale !

See how its folds o'er vassel hills
　　Float in their starry sheen,
The Pike's Peak Flag !　The mountain flag !
　　The highest earth hath seen !

VI.

Look forth upon these moss-grown rocks,
　　Of pink and spangled gold,
This peak stupendous, hoar with age,
　　" Above a world unrolled."
The sentinel of earth and sky,
　　Lord of eternal snows,
The monarch of the Rocky Range,
　　Its awful summit shows.

VII.

The sinking sun in crimson flames
　　The farther hills forsakes,
And opalescent shifting lights
　　Dance on the placid lakes,
The rose and purple vapors creep
　　Up Cameron's craggy cone,
And we must leave our eyrie high
　　To silence on her throne !

VIII.

A lingering look where Denver lies,
　　Then South Park's lovely vale,

On Rocky Mountain's white-capped chain,
  Then down the rugged "trail,"
To Colorado's lofty peak,
  We bid a last adieu!
Good-bye to lonely signal staff,
  And mount for Manitou!

U. S. Signal Station, Pike's Peak, Col. July 22, 1886.

NAPOLEON. (2)

ALONE he stands upon the rugged shore,
    Where beats the spray, 'mid sullen breaker's
      roar.
The ocean waves dash o'er the rocks in foam,
And howling surge around his island home.
Far off are phantom sails which mock his sight
And glide away in endless lines of light.
Day follows day, and darkness comes and goes,
Alone he lives amid his hated foes.
Yet proud and stern, he gives no sign of pain,
The cruel jailer's taunts are all in vain.
Down, down where scoundrels in perdition lie
Let Lowe's base memory forever die.
While as the eternal cycles roll along,
Napoleon still the theme of Gallic song,
Shall live triumphant on historic pages,
The greatest man of all recorded ages.
For nature made but one—then broke the mould,
All else is silver, *this* was purest gold.
And all the malice, spleen and petty spite
But show the hero in a brighter light,
To glow and strengthen as the years increase,
Nor fade or pale *'til Time itself shall cease.*

OH, LASSIE, DOST THOU FEAR
THE SEA? (3)

I.

OH, Lassie, dost thou fear the sea,
    The crawling hungry foam,
And dost thou sigh for crested hills
    Of far off Highland home?
Oh, wild and fierce the savage sea,
    Though waves have wooing tones,
So purrs the tiger o'er its prey
    Yet crunches still thy bones.

II.

The mountains give their children lost,
    The berries of the glen,
The water from their crystal springs,
    The sympathies of men.
The *feline* sea will lick thy feet
    With lips of crimson hue,
Will mock thy thirst with cruel taunts,
    To die in waters blue.

III.

Oh, Lassie, dost thou love the hills,
    The tranquil hills and vales,
When gazing on the snaky sea,
    As it smooths its silver scales?
Thou can'st not see the close knit joints,
    Or gleaming serpent sever.
Dost hear its weird and haunting song,
    Forever and forever!
The dreary, weary monotone
    Eternal—aye—forever!

IV.

Oh, Lassie, dost thou fear the sea,
    Dost hear the dirge sublime,
Now drowning human anthems out,
    Now crushing human time?
Oh, hearts of love in granite hills,
    Oh, mountains of delight,
How do ye dwarf all petty thoughts
    In thy grim and awful might?

V.

Oh, Lassie, dost thou fear the sea,
    With endless surging tide,
And dost thou hear the Gnome king's cry,
    As he seeketh earthly bride?

Oh, Lassie, far are Highland hills,—
  The Basilisk is near,
Now soft its note—now loud its roar,
  Comes thundering in thine ear.

VI.

Oh, Lassie, dost thou fear the sea?
  With emerald circled brow,
The sapphire curls o'er gleaming face,
  Where thou art gazing now.
So charmeth Vishnu Bramah's God,
  By Delhi's templed steep,
So Vampires foul with soothing wings,
  Their victims lull to sleep.

VII.

Oh, Lassie, dost thou fear the sea,
  Dost dread its summer smiles,
Dost fear the storms and dragon's breath
  The webs and tempting wiles?
Hast thou, dear Lass, the key to those,
  Who sea-like fawn forever.
But treacherous are as slimy depths,
  Oh, trust them not, oh, never;
Their smiling, purring dulcet tone,
  Oh, heed it not forever.

WHERE THE ASPENS BLOW.

THE glorious evenings of long ago,
  Still come with the shimmering stars of night,
On the lawns as of old the Aspens blow,
  With quivering leaves in the trembling light,
And the clear sounds come from the mid-air zone,
  In mellow notes to the listening ear,
Ringing and singing an old, old tone,
  Of evenings gone—*still* lingering here.

And the red-orbed mornings of long ago
  Still come with the radiant eyes of love.
On the hills as of old, the purple glow
  Of the rushing dawn in the skies above—
And still in the noon, in the hot sunshine,
  The quivering leaves of the Aspen blow,
And evening and morning and noon are thine,
  Thine in the present—as in days long ago.

To-day and to-morrow in spaceless time,
  In the glare of the sun, or moonlight pale,
Thou shalt live forever in golden prime
  While the heart keeps young, though the senses
    fail.

Forever and ever to you shall be
  The glorious evening of long ago,
Forever the beauty on grassy lea,
  Where the trembling leaves of the Aspen blow.

Yes, morning and evening in dream-land fair,
  Thou must not live for thyself alone !
Lest all beauty shall fade from earth and air,
  And vanish forever the old, old tone !
Let us walk through life, in its pleasant vales,
  And search the wonders of the peerless sky,
Tell over and over the old, old tales,
  Tales learned in a youth which shall never die.

A REMINISCENCE OF MANITOU.

A ND we had crossed the prairies wide,
    Had scaled the snowy mountain
And rambled through fair Manitou,
    Beside the bubbling Fountain ;
The days were bright, and blue the skies,
    The landscape like a dream—
The days we strolled in Manitou,
    Fast by the boiling stream.

The dashing waters sparkling flow
    Adown the rocky glen,
In rainbow falls from tinted cliffs
    To-day as they did then.
The red vines trail o'er mossy steeps
    And cañon paths invite
To nooks and caves and crystal lakes,
    Which charm us with delight.

Remember from the rustic bridge
    We gazed upon the peak,
Encircled in a cloud of storms,
    With hearts too awed to speak ;

And by the Fountain's currents
　　We vowed beneath the sky
To stand upon the summit,
　　Or in its thunders die.

And how, when summer faded
　　On the mesas brown and gray,
We turned our steps from Manitou
　　And went our wandering way :
And how we left our stranger friends
　　Still 'neath the snowy mountain,
And drank adieu's from bubbling springs
　　Beside the river Fountain.

Does nature still in purity
　　Her robes trail o'er the Fountain,
And still provide the woody glens
　　In rifts within the mountain ?
And could we now at Manitou,
　　As in the days of yore,
Find still the wierd and magic scenes
　　Amid its wealth galore ?

Or would we find in fashion's throng
　　And fashion's stilted tone,
The charms which nature gave us
　　When nature held her own ?

And will our eyes ere rest again
   Upon the snowy mountain ?
And can we feel as on that day
   On bridge 'o'er boiling Fountain ?

And will we take a palace car
   To top off hoary mountain,
Where once we climbed its craggy sides
   From base beside the Fountain ?
Or backward shall our vision turn
   To days that are no more,
When nature held her court alone
   Beside the Fountain's shore ?

PUEBLO. (5)

THE Arkansaw forever,
  With its waters of unrest,
Shall trail the course of empire
  To the Pittsburg of the West,
With furnace roar, and smelters' flow,
  Of seething molton ore,
And mines of coal and tons of steel,
  And cattle kings galore.

In the basin in the valley,
  In the pathway traced by fate,
From Atlantic to Pacific,
  And glowing Golden Gate,
Sits this city of Pueblo,
  With skies of Syrian sheen,
Encircled by the treasure hills,
  The Rocky Mountain Queen.

Not of thy skies so clear and pure,
  Of cañon, cave or glen,
Of cataract or grass or flower,
  Or armied workingmen,

Of long lost races—idols rude
　Of shrines forever broken,
Or Colorado's golden stores
　Are memories unspoken.

No, not of gold or silver,
　Of mines, or ranch or plain,
Nor mystic scenes of fairy-land,
　Cometh the weird refrain,
Which sings to the heart its music,
　And the voice doth ever call
To the mind, the forms of those who wait
　Where mountain shadows fall.

And these voices o'er Pueblo,
　How strange that it should be
That the circle of the mountains
　Draws wondrous near to me,
From their treasures heaped and shining,
　And their gems beyond compare,
In the valley of the Fountain,
　Where the gentle murmurs are.

From Green Horn's vista'd summits,
　From blue capped Peaks of Spain
There cometh o'er Pueblo
　The gentle, low refrain—

Across the verdured Mesa,
In the sunny laden air,
The echoes from the ranges
Are floating in a prayer.

And the hills beyond Pueblo,
How near to me they seem,
The snow that lies upon their sides,
I see its distant gleam,
And nearer still and nearer
Shall *Sangre de Cristo* shine
Whose shadows fall this starry night
On other eyes than mine.

Eyes turned in earnest longing,
On the ever wooing peak
With a strangeness overcoming
And words they can not speak,
Where flows the Fountain River
In its currents to the sea,
Those eyes in far Pueblo
Are near and dear to me.

Hillsboro, O., March 1, 1888.

VESPERS. (6)

A LONE upon this tufted hill
   In silence, while the air
Is pulseless, all is still, so still,
   You feel no presence there.
But hark, from distant village tow'r
   Saint Mary's gentle strain
Proclaims the blessed vesper hour,—
   Tired Labor rests again.

The mellowed tones, in liquid chime,
   Fall on the list'ning ear;
Down drop the spades, comes vesper time,
   Then home with all its cheer.
O! weary life, with short respite,
   All work and restless brain;
For labor hard each morn's red light
   Brings fast upon its train.

The sun's last rays from western sky
   Glint on St. Mary's spire;
The cross, all golden, sparkles high
   With streams of burnished fire.

Great bars of purple and yellow light
　　Reach to the zenith blue,
As day fades into sullen night,
　　Show dying dolphins' hue.

All ripened are the glowing fields,
　　Soft falls the dew on earth ;
We see the fruitful harvest yields,
　　For labor gave it birth.
From sheltered nooks the cabin fires
　　Ascending, make us feel
That woman's hand, which never tires,
　　Prepares the evening meal.

By coverts close, and brook-side lone,
　　The cattle stand in peace,
And twilight beetles' soothing drone
　　Now murmurs, Labor, cease ;
On dusty road, far, far below,
　　The trav'lers hurry by,
Like phantom horsemen flitting go,
　　Where home and pleasures lie.

O blessed, blessed eventide,
　　When vesper hymns arise,
And Labor lays its toils aside, ·
　　And turns to God its eyes ;

Who has not felt in this sweet hour,
  Whate'er his trials were,
That time would come, no earthly power,
  Could bring again despair?

THE ORIOLE. ⁽⁷⁾

HAUNTER of the orchard,
  Singing clear and free,
Flitting o'er the green sward,
  Full of melody,
Where the apple blossoms, or buds the tulip tree.

In the blush of morning,
  In the evening gray,
Ever still adorning
  All the Summer's day,
From thy airy mansion, with the winds at play.

Challenging the plough boy,
  "Whistling his team afield,"
With thy matin song of joy,
  All his sense to yield
To the mocking banter, from bending willow shield.

Flecked in brightest yellow,
  Helmeted in black,
Piping thy whistle mellow,
  Glancing on his track,
Like a gnome or fairy, tempting answer back.

34

Delicate vermillion,
　　Dancing on the sight,
　　Deepest tinge of orange
　　In thy plumage bright,
Lend beauty to the foliage, and sparkle in the light.

These are the colors olden,
　　Of lordly Baltimore,
　　Flashed by the Fire-bird golden,
　　Upon our western shore,
And giving thee a title,　which noble Calverts bore.

Among the branches gleaming,
　　This heraldic coat of arms,
　　Like ancient banner streaming,
　　But adds unto thy charms,
Linked with the noble Calverts and Indian alarms.

The Baltimores are sleeping,
　　The sponsors of thy name,
　　But *thy* presence still is keeping,
　　Eternally their fame,
Undying and immortal, like Roman Vestal's flame.

BY THE MOUNTAIN AND THE SHORE.

WHERE the dreamy waters murmured,
    Fleck'd with gold and amber hued,
'Midst the phantom shadows stealing,
    From the copse of birchen wood ;
Where the green waves, fondly dashing,
    Beat the shore in circlets nigh,
Stood at eve a sparkling maiden,
    Light her heart, and bright her eye.

Mute beside the glassy river,
    Twilight shading wood and sky,
Here 'twere joy to live forever—
    In the forests live and die ;
Where the waves, each other chasing,
    Bathe the sedge upon the shore,
Dwell upon this fairy margin
    In the glen forevermore.

"A penny for your thoughts," young tourist,
    Ere these magic scenes depart ;
Shall regrets forever haunt thee,
    Dim the eye and cloud the heart ;

Fairy glen and dancing river,
  Tangled path beside the shore,
Melt away from earthly vision,
  Memories, and nothing more.

Then her mouth with smiles was kindled,
  Laughter floated on the breeze,
As she coaxing called upon me,
  " Write some poetry, won't you, please ? "
The evening wind was gently rust'ling
  Through the daisies wet with dew,
The yellow stars were dimly peeping
  O'er the mountain's crest of blue.

Shall I write a goblin story,
  Legend old with horrors fraught,
While the hoary mountains beckon
  Themes from out the world of thought ?
Or, shall laughter fright the spectres,
  Wailing in the mournful pines,
And the echo of thy spirit,
  Ring the measure of the lines ?

Thou must leave the rippling waters
  Where the twilight trembling stays,
Emerald Pool and frowning mountains
  Be a thought of vanished days.

Yet will fancy sometimes linger
  On the mountains grim and hoar,
Formed by HIM who keepeth ever
  Watch and ward beside the shore.

Gilded hours are swiftly passing
  By the crystal hills and streams,
And our tourist rounds of pleasure
  Soon will be but idle dreams ;
Still the elfin lamps will glitter
  On these purple rocks below,
Still the azure dome of heaven
  Will with starlight be aglow.

Radiant morning hence shall lead thee,
  And the night shall lull to sleep,
By rocky coast and beaches sandy,
  To the music of the deep.
May HE whose temples are the hills,
  Whose shrines are by the shore,
Watch o'er this wand'ring tourist fair,
  Whose billows ceaseless roar.

Soon thou shalt see the red-orbed sun
  From ocean waters rise,
With flaming pennons floating far
  Athwart the eastern skies ;

And mark the change to golden hue,
　As, springing from the waves,
The day-god drives his chariot
　From Neptune's coral caves.

And thou shalt see his lances gleam
　Far as the eye can reach,
As, tinged in foam, the white-caps break
　On Nahant's shell-girt beach.
And thou shalt see, when perfect day
　Is cloudless in the light,
The fair and distant sails go by,
　Like phantoms dim and white.

And thou shall stand where surging tides
　On rocks eternal beat,
And cast the treasures of the sea
　Beneath thy wandering feet ;
And strange and far these hills will be,
　Whose summits on us peer,
While near and clear the ocean's roar
　Is thundering in the air.

Lake and river, glen and mountain,
　Ocean, cave, and tide-washed strand,
Forms of beauty, shapes of wonder,
　Fashioned by an all-wise hand,

Wheresoe'er thy fate may lead thee,
   Sheltered in HIS strong embrace,
May no blight of care or sorrow
   Darkly shadow thy young face.

And when other scenes and places
   Drive from thought this magic glen,
Keep this council traced sincerely,
   By a fellow-pilgrim's pen :
Keep, O keep, in wood or city,
   In the crowd, or when alone,
Keep, O keep thy joyous nature,
   ' Tis a treasure, all thine own.

MIDNIGHT IN THE GLEN.

(INSCRIBED TO MY DAUGHTER NELLIE.)

Spirits with:

> ——"haunts in dale or piny mountain,
> Or forest by slow stream or pebbly spring,
> Or chasms and watery depths,"
> ——*The Piccolomini.*

I.

A T midnight, in a cloudless sky,
    The climbing moon uprose,
On somber vales and glassy brooks
    Its mellow color throws ;
Now resting in the lines of light,
    Now dancing o'er the rills,
Fantastic shapes and gleaming sprites
    Are flitting in the hills.

II.

The bright-eyed deer, with graceful bound,
    Stop near the limpid streams
To gaze upon their beauty fair,
    Reflected by the beams.

By mountain trees that cluster o'er
    The tranquil, silent lake,
The wand'ring eagle furls his wings,
    While night-birds are awake.

III.

The trout, swift-swimming through the wave,
    Gay tenant of the stream,
Has plunged into its hidden depths,
    And vanished like a dream ;
And now on couch of radiant shells,
    Forgets the coming day,
When from the wanton wave he leaps,
    The cruel angler's prey,
And all that breathed, or all that moved,
    Had sought their place of rest ;
The night was calm, and still, and fair,
    In golden colors dressed.

IV.

But hark ! a swell of murmurs strange,
    From coverts in the hills,
Deep as an organ's volumed tone,
    The night-air slowly fills ;
And now it rises, dirge-like note,
    Unto the cloudless blue,
The midnight song of mountain fays,
    And Gnomes of dusty hue ;

For there are forest fairies here,
  Who from the caverned shades
Come forth and hold their revels loud,
  In lonely mountain glades.
Upon the snowy giant's crown,
  As hand in hand they go,
The phantom host in festal glee
  Leer down on us below.
They scowl at all that's innocent,
  Enchanters of the wood,
And try, by all the tempter's art,
  To overcome the good.
O step not in their magic ring,
  At midnight in the glen,
Or shining glamour fades away—
  Thou art the demons' then !
Hear not the mountain's clear cut chime,
  Nor listen to its moan,
Nor search its hidden rocks of gold,
  When night is on her throne.

v.

But still the blue sky smiles above,
  So saintly and so fair,
And wild flowers whisper as they hear
  These voices of the air.
Soft voices charm to dreams unsought,
  In nature's temples then,

And in the valley all is peace,
　　At midnight in the glen.
There is an eye, by day or night,
　　Its vigils still will keep,
On mountain crest and valley lone,
　　Where mortals weary sleep;
So thou but trust thine all to Him,
　　And to His words be true,
Nor mountain sprite, nor midnight Gnome,
　　Can harm bring unto you.

WHITE MOUNTAINS, July, 1882.

THE LUXEMBOURG. (9)

(TO MY COUSIN, MRS. F. W. ARMSTRONG, PARIS,
JULY 21, 1883.)

WE saw the Sculptor's art in stone,
　　And cunning skill in bronze and gold :—
From painted canvas on us shone
　　The Heroines of ages old.
The faultless form, the classic face,
　　The soul which glows in passion there ;
The nameless charm, the high-born grace,
　　Which makes each lady seem so fair.

The roses bloom, the fountains play.
　　Serene and cold, in marble grand,
The Queens who ruled in by-gone day
　　Illustrious on the Terrace stand,—
Marguerite de Provence, proud and fair,
　　Marguerite de Valois, false and vain ;
Marguerite Splendid, of Navarre,
　　Marguerite of Anjou, doomed to pain.

The Troubadour their praises sung,
　　The armored knight set lance at rest ;
Great Princes on their accents hung,—
　　To die for them was to be blest.

45

For them the tocsin called to war,
  The soldier lonely vigils kept ;
The moon from sky, in Crescent car,
  Smiled on the spot where Beauty slept.

Where gleams the Lake in shadow *there*,
  A school-boy stooped his head to lave ;
Or on yon seat, when free from care,
  He gazed at Tritons in the wave.
Where giant trees o'erspread the lawn,
  So *then*, as *now*, in regal state,
These marble Queens—that sculptured Faun,
  A Cupid *here* and *there* a Fate.

Beneath the same deep azure sky
  His path lay *here*—in boyish glee
To studies *then ;* but *now* a tie
  Still stronger binds his life to thee !
With modest thought, and gentle creed,
  O study well each other's weal,
Which pulseless Hebes do not heed,
  Or stately Courtiers think or feel.

And turn from all these gems of Art,
  To husband, daughter, near and dear,
And kinsman's warm and friendly heart,
  Which envies not the splendor here.

For in these Gardens, once of Eld,
   This haughty Lord, *that* jeweled Dame,
Their gilded revels nightly held,
   While France lay reeking in its shame.

For thee a nobler lyric crown,
   It can not deck a fairer brow ;
May Time press lightly with his frown
   Where youth and sunshine cluster now.
And when is reached Eternal seas,
   And sullen tempest's moaning roar,
May HE who calms the rising breeze,
   Guide thee and thine to Golden Shore.

In Highland Hills, in gladsome Spring,
   While bubbling waters soothe the ear,
At Winter eve will memory bring
   Again these scenes which linger here.
The sculptured forms in dreams will rise,
   This charming music make refrain ;
These phantoms pass before the eyes,—
   The Luxembourg return again.

THE MISANTHROPE.

"Homo sum, et humani, a me nil alienum puto."
—*Terence.*

I.

SOLITARY 'mid all this stir of busy life ; alone,
   He treads this pleasant earth a stranger to its
   joys unknown,
For him no woman's love, no friendly grasp of
   neighbor's hand,
No children's smiles, no mother's kiss—this wanderer in the land ;
No mourning tears by him are dried, no sorrow fills
   the breast
Where selfish misery holds its court, and soul is at
   unrest ;
When suffering lies along his path, he turns in
   sullen pride,
And, like the Levite and the Priest, "he takes the
   other side."

II.

Apart in gloomy state he walks, nor mingles with
   his kind,
The road long pressed by human feet suits not his
   morbid mind ;

48

No play for him, no sports allure, earth is a desert
    wild ;
Man loves him not as he hates man ; O was he e'er
    a child ?
Or did great Nature, in his case, reverse her
    common rule,
And mark him with the brand of Cain—this solitary
    fool ?
To dwell in desolation's halls, unknowing and
    unknown,
Despising and despised, to walk, his selfish path
    alone.

III.

O seek for pleasure in this life, as swiftly pass the
    years,
Take interest in your fellow-men, their hopes, their
    plans, their fears ;
Read of the men whose monuments are builded in
    the heart,
Their speculations, goodly schemes, where man-
    kind took a part.
In business, love, or politics, the golden moments
    fly,
The busy man finds beauty still in earth, in air, in
    sky ;

Or if you choose in Fashion's throng, or churches'
     graver tone,
Go mingle with the human crowd who do not live
     alone.

IV.

Why lingers here this Ishmaelite? What is his
     final goal ;
And will he always be alone, this miserable soul ?
And still contemn our pleasant world, when in the
     silent land
No tidal wave can cast him back upon this hated
     strand ?
Will he regret, upon that shore, the traveler's final
     bourne ?
No feeling heart upon this globe for him doth weep
     or mourn ;
And will he, in Elysian fields, still wander all
     unknown,
'Mid multitudes of buried dead, still tread his path
     alone ?

THE WANING YEAR

WE walk together down the slopes of Time,
    The fading year and I,
'Till midnight bells ring out their morning chime,
    We will not say good-bye.

We have been friends by mountain, sea and shore,
    The passing year and I,
In fleeting days that now can come no more,
    On sun-lit earth and sky.

When we shall part let smiles, not tears, have
        sway—
    There is good reason why,
What blessings gathered 'round our devious way,
    None know but you and I.

What trysts we kept and how we held our trust,
    The waning year and I,
Shall sleep forgotten in the mingled dust,
    Of centuries gone by.

"What's writ is writ," but scanty fields are won,
    Although our aims were high.
What we have hoped to do, yet left undone,
    With you, old year, must die.

December, 1891.

THE ABBEY OF SAINT DENIS.

FRANCE.

HERE lie the kings of ages past,
   'Neath this old Abbey's Fane ;
In shapeless heap their bones are cast,
   Like war's unburied slain.
Here *once* their plumes in triumph waved
   In bright and fair array ;
Nought *now* but names, on tablets graved,
   But kings ! O where are they?

The morning mist is floating o'er
   This strangest spot in France,
The shoes of wood now pace the floor
   Where rattled shield and lance ;
From Dagobert and Charlemagne,
   To Bourbon's awful fate,
They sleep, these kings, no grief or pain,
   In dreamless silent state.

The centuries have darkly passed,
   So boundless in their sway,
Since Charlemagne's shrill trumpet blast
   Made listening slaves obey.

The conquering chief his helmet doffs,
   The brandished scepter falls,
And silence reigns where vassal shouts
   Rang through the festal halls.

O curtained Past ! O mystic Past !
   How weird this place appears,
Where sculptured kings, in marble cast,
   Recall the vanished years.
The dim Church flame in mockery throws
   Its light on hopeless gloom,
A taper's faint and flickering ray
   On every kingly tomb.

From Clovis fierce to Louis grand
   The Dead are here inurned,
Each slumbrous form with folded hand
   And face to heaven turned.
Beneath these vaults, and Abbey dome,
   Immortal spirits throng ;
Wild Fancy here can make its home,
   And Poets weave their song.

Unrolled the Ages spectral fly
   With boding raven's wing ;
The clustering shades, in moaning sigh,
   Around our footsteps cling.

Cathedral lone, hold fast your gloom
Where kings in slumber lie ;
Let all who wish muse on the Tomb,
Give me the sunlit sky.

GOOD BY. ⁽¹⁰⁾

I.

GOOD by to the Island,
   Green Erin, good by :
To the mists on Killarney,
   The blue in thy sky,
To inlets and havens,
   The rocks on thy coast ;
Thy true-hearted people,
   Of nations the boast.

II.

Good by to Cork harbor,
   Where navies may ride
When storms stir the ocean
   In anger and pride.
As fogs gather 'round us,
   'Mid tempest's harsh roar,
As ship leaves the offing,
   My heart is on shore.

III.

And faith is unshaken,
  That yet the red hand
Of Vengeance will loosen
  The chains from the land.
O where is the siren
  With Liberty's smile ?
O why has she slighted
  This sea-circled isle ?

IV.

O sleeping or waking,
  Wherever thou art,
The tears that are flowing
  Appeal to thy heart.
May Freedom then hasten
  The treasure to save,
And Erin will trample
  On tyranny's grave.

V.

The signal is given,
  The flag at the mast,
The farewells are spoken,—
  With many the last !
The ship has weighed anchor,
  The soul breathes a sigh ;
In sorrow and silence,
  O Erin, good by !

THE HIGHLAND HILLS.

FAIR glows the morn on Highland Hills,
   How glad the sunshine beams !
How green the slopes in Summer dress,
   By Highland's pleasant streams !
Why stay so long by household gate,
   The parting word to speak ?
What means this fullness of the heart,
   This dampness on the cheek ?

'Tis done ! Farewell to wife and home ;
   Regrets are now in vain ;
Let memory have her perfect work,
   O'er mind, and heart and brain.
Farewell, the rock-ribbed Highland Hills,
   Each stream, and field and tree,
Nor still forget this Highland home,
   When far away at sea !

When fading hues of native shore
   Pass from the lingering sight,
And, round are swirling ocean waves,
   In mid-Atlantic's night ;

When language strange and customs rude
    Assail the eye and ear,
Turn in the silent realms of thought
    To Highland Hills so dear.

Know ye beneath those craggy hills,
    And on their sunny slopes,
Are family, friends and household gods,
    And all your *earthly* hopes.
Nor time, nor tide, nor lands, nor seas,
    Nor foreign cities grand,
Can dim the love of Highland Home,
    Where hills of Highland stand.

THE EMERALD ISLE.

WE sailed around the sea-girt isle
　　One Summer afternoon ;
The ocean seemed on us to smile,
　　That happy day in June.

And all is silent 'neath the sky,
　　Nor sound of voices there,
But white-gull's shrill and piping cry
　　Upon the ocean air.

Can we forget this lovely day,
　　This green and rugged shore,
When first we saw the Irish Land,
　　Then part to meet no more ?

Can time or tide or poet's lay,
　　Or seas which on us smile,
Make each or all forget this day
　　We coast the Emerald Isle ?

How fair our skies, how bright the sun,
　　This golden Summer day,
With Hope's firm " Anchor " at her brow,
　　" Belgravia " rides the bay.

O ! Faith's firm " Anchor," emblem fit
  To brace the mourning heart ;
May every soul on this proud ship
  From this faith never part.

The gilded hours went swiftly by
  As o'er Atlantic tides,
'Mid music, song, and spirits light,
  Our vessel safely glides.

Now fair the seas, and short the hours,
  'Till landed at our port ;
We are at home in Irish waves,
  When anchor's penants float.

We see the verdured Irish coast,
  And Albion's haughty strand ;
Do not forget *our home* at sea,
  When anchored on the land.

Soon we must part : O where to wander,
  Where to meet, ah ! who can tell ?
Are you ready for the summons ?
  Can you tell us " all is well ? "

Green will be this charming island,
  When thou and I, and all are gone,
And the ocean still forever
  Sing its mournful monotone.

The seaweed still shall drift in foam,
  And Dolphins change their hue,
And Nautilus spread its purple sail
  'Mid waters green and blue.

And other eyes shall idly gaze
  Where sky and ocean meet,
While 'round them spreads the wide, wide sea,
  A good ship 'neath their feet.

Farewell to Red-Cross flag at mast,
  Our emblem day by day ;
On English soil we still will think
  Of our sailing up the bay.

ERIN. (II)

AS REPRESENTED IN ART.

WHO is she now gazing
    Across the dark sea,
With girdle unloosened,
    And hair flowing free?
With hand on her forehead,
    And feet in the wave,
Ariadne or Erin,
    Can she be a slave?

The light-house is gleaming
    'Mid shoals on the shore,
The ship is now dashing
    'Mid breakers dull roar.
O why does she linger?
    How long shall she wait?
O tell us, dear Echo,
    What shall be her fate?

The sad years are passing,
    Her face has grown pale,
With traces of sorrow,
    O will her hope fail?

As gazing, still gazing,
   Where sun sinks to rest,
For the true Prince in armor,
   From out of the west.

I STROLLED, a stranger, on a Summer night,
  Along the Boulevard, with its lines of light
And glamour gleaming on this fairy-land,
With gilded phantoms gliding hand in hand,
From shining depths to far horizon blue,
Were dancing flames of many colored hue.
No darkness here, but such a radiance, fair
As August suns, flood mid-noon's Gallic air;
The shadows creep and hide in dismal courts,
And leave the Boulevard to its festive sports.
These revelers see no pall or gloomy shroud,
But gaily prattle in the thronging crowd.
They hear no distant booming of the bell,
With sullen tone from vestibule of Hell.
With *no* belief, these creatures of a day,
When life is o'er, return again to clay.
Death ends it all, and so they pass along,
Enwreathed in pleasure, wine and song.
Here all is magic, and the flashing eye
Sees not that all this gaudy life must die.
No ear is turned to where sad labor groans,
And no heart throbs at misery's feeble moans;

No voice is heard to cast a warning chill,
Bid pleasure cease and signal future ill,
For these "are to the manner born," while we
Live in a far-off land beyond the sea.
As strangers we may muse, and idly gaze
At novel sights in wonder and amaze ;
As strangers join these "mummers" face to face,
And learn by practice all their ease and grace.
These smiles are false, and but an actor's part,
They charm the sense, but leave untouched the
    heart.
You look in vain for something good or true,
And do at last as all the others do.
Beware lest tempters in their nets enthrall
A soul forgetful of its duty's call.
'Tis three A. M., and waiting morn now peers
O'er the gay capital, which idly jeers
And still carouses with a ceaseless din,—
An earthly Pandemonium of sin.
The dashing Voiture with its coursers fleet,
And jeweled Houris flits along the street ;
And coaches rattle 'mid the dazzling sheen
Of radiant vistas in the foliage green.
Through glowing panes shine wondrous works of
    art,
The spell of beauty to a tourist's heart.
'Neath arches, where the Sculptures nobly trace
Triumphant trophies of a by-gone race ;
By Columns on whose storied summits stand

The heroes who have glorified the land ;
By Cafés, where many a table bright
Jingles with glasses through the waning night ;
By Ancient Gates we pass in dreams along,
And passages filled with mirth and song,
Where fair are all things, and how glad and free
Seem those who mingle in these scenes of glee.
Do these Blue-Blouses flitting here and there,
Who seem in all this phantom life to share,
Deep in their souls have keen desire to slay?
And do they wander here in search of prey?
Are victims marked by Fauborg, Saint Antoine,
When Blouse shall rise to claim again his own?
When from alleys dark, and dismal den,
Shall surge a murderous mob of starving men !
Is there beneath this pageant's hollow show
Volcanic fires which in their embers glow?
Will Commune dread o'er Paris once more rise,
With terror burning in its lurid eyes?
Shall Columns fall 'neath desolation's tread,
And Palaces crumble with their weight of dead?
While fire shall waste these avenues and stalk
Resistless through each pleasant Summer walk,
Shall strangers search 'mid ruins, grim and bare,
For Eglise Madeleine with its saintly air,
Or Arc de Triomphe, Obelisk, or Fane
Of Notre Dame, and find their search in vain?
'Mid wreck of Revolution's ghastly shroud,
Which broods o'er Paris in a sullen cloud,

Will aught remain, except where proudly stands
The July Column, reared by Freedom's hands?
Whose sandaled Hermes overlooks the place
Where fell the Bastile in its deep disgrace;
'Tis on this spot, the despot's gloomy grave,
No Frenchman feels he e'er can be a slave.
Here ends our stroll, while Nemesis is dead,
And all the maskers nothing yet may dread;
To them all vows are false, all virtue lost,
And man upon a hopeless current tossed;
They know not home, nor kith, nor kind, nor kin
Amid this tapestry of gilded sin.
We, strolling strangers, lookers-on, alone,
Have something solid we may call our own,
And turn in gladness to the western sun,
In coming twilight when its course is run;
We see it sink to rest, and evening star
Stands trembling o'er a wave-washed land afar;
We think not, care not, for the ocean foam,
As thoughts go rushing to our far-off home.

PARIS, FRANCE, August, 1883.

COMING HOME.

I.

THE headlands have vanished,
　　No beacons in sight,
O'er wide wasting billows
　　We plunge into night.
The wind, how it mutters,
　　And dashes the foam !
So farewell to Europe,
　　The West is our home.

II.

The ocean is sullen,
　　The mad waves are high,
The lightning is gleaming
　　Athwart the black sky ;
We care not and fear not,
　　And calmly can rest,
While proudly the good ship
　　Sails into the West.

III.

And welcome each morrow,
   Though fog may prevail ;
Let billows surround us
   And fierce blow the gale,
Each gloom-darkened even
   Has marked on the chart
The leagues we have measured
   To home of the heart.

IV.

And nearer, still nearer,
   Till bathed in the light,
The star-spangled emblem
   Is flashed on the sight.
One moment we linger,
   The Tender has come ;
Farewell to the ocean,
   And welcome our home.

INUENDO.

DID you see that sneer?
It spoke a puppy's small soul slighted,
Whose shallow hopes the lady blighted,
Now passing near.

A poisoned smile
Suggesting *that*, he dare not speak,
But leaves a meaning which you seek,—
The lady's vile.

A scoundrel's leer,
Which seems to say, as she passed along,
In this craven mood of hinting wrong,
She is not pure.

He thinks it scorn ;—
'Tis but a coward's sneaking ire,
While envy burns his soul with fire,
Of malice born.

A hint, a breath,
Insinuating *that* or *this*,—
With venom of a serpent's hiss,
Producing death.

A point, a sign,
A meaning shrug, a hint obscure,
To sully those whom God made pure,—
   The sex divine.

This human crow
Looks not like eagle to the sky,
But turns to earth with leering eye,
   For something low.

A vampire foul,
A carrion ghoul, a social spot,
A crawling, creeping, wretched blot,—
   Base slander's tool.

The voice is hushed,
But in the look pollution lies;
'Gainst virtue every feature cries,
   And it is crushed!

A blur, a stain
On mother, daughter, wife and sister;
May all in Hades scorch and blister
   Who give each pain.

CHRISTMAS DIALECTICS.

I.

IS the world any wiser because it is older,
  The women more lovely, the men any bolder?
Do friends of our race keep the text to the letter,
Commissioned on earth to make us all better?
Is there anything true, or is it *ideal*,
And who can distinguish the false from the real?
Are all our beliefs but mere matters of doubt,
And the faiths of our childhood "turned inside
    out?"
Agnostics take pleasure because they *don't* know
The wherefore of things above or below,
Contented as atoms which float in the air,
Inspired by no faith and depressed by no care,
The existence of God neither assert or deny,
Take things as they are, without asking "the why?"
Religion is right, or wrong, as you choose,
They do not accept, nor do they refuse.

II.

Ignoramus in Latin, *Agnostic* in Greek,
To find what is truth you have only to seek.

" Who seeks me shall find me " was stated of yore,
By one who then spake as no man had before.
Admit there is something that never can die,
And the " wherefore " is plain, the reason, and
  " why ? "
If science proves anything, it clearly has shown
The universe governed by rules of its own,
Underlying all nature a *purpose* and law,
Consistent, and fixed without error or flaw.
The truth it impresses, o'ertopping the whole,
Conclusively teaches the life of the soul.
Thus the question is answered " *For what are we*
  here ? "
The *premise* admitted, the solution is clear.
If our physical death is the end here below,
Then indeed all is vain and " nothing we know."

III.

As the world waxeth old, it becometh more sage,
As wine in its casket is mellowed by age.
The women are fairer than stories have told.
The men more courageous than heroes of old,
And friends of our race believe in the text—
Good done in *this* world will count in the next.
There are many things true as well as i-de-al,
And 'tis easy to tell the false from the real.
The faith of the fathers however we scout,
To many is firm and unshaken by doubt,

And still live the children whose curious eyes
Scan the beauties of earth and the blue of the skies.
Believers take comfort because they *do* know,
The promise of heaven is for mortals below.
Not atoms all aimless that shift with earth's air,
They cherish their hopes and unburthen their care.
That "God lives and reigns" they feel and they
     know,
As their fathers did in the long ago.
The God who from the whirlwind and the cloud,
Proclaimed eternal truth in tones aloud,
And on the far Idumean plain
Rebuked the Temanite for his questionings vain.
They know the speculations of the Eastern sages
Had drifted slowly down successive ages,
Until *One* came who solved for each or all,
The Roman Pilate's problem in the judgment hall.
While time shall last, and living things have birth,
The truth there spoken shall not cease from earth.

    December, 1891.

THE "HIGHLAND WILDS."

ALL through the tangled thicket lair,
    Where Paint Creek waters rapid flow,
We comrades, blithe and debonair,
    Tramped bravely several moons ago.
The morns were clear—before the sight
    Far spread a leafy girdled zone
Of forest giants in the light
    Of dawn upon her purple throne.

We searched the caves, in gorges hidden
    The secrets dread of wood and wold,
And "flashed the light" on things forbidden,
    And wierd enchantments yet untold.
The caverned depths give up their gloom,
    To distant nooks the shadows fly,
The camera types the crystal room
    In splendor to the curious eye.

The far off clouds in **August days**,
    Were banked in many a dome and spire,
The red-orbed sun in parching rays
    Shone on the cliffs with eye of fire.

When noons were still and skies were warm,
   And soft the mountain zephyrs blew,
While nature showed us every charm,
   From camera plates the pictures drew.

From "Highland Wilds" the Club have gone,
   Their August tryst was not in vain,
It lingers in remembered tone
   Where beauty tints the hill and plain.
The Club still tramps the Highland vales,
   Still catch the types of earth and sky,
Still tell again the old, old tales
   Born of a tryst that can not die.

Still walks the Club o'er grassy lea
   While summers come and summers go,
And the tryst of the Eight will ever be
   A dream where the rapid waters flow.
No spot forgotten—nor the time
   By gleaming sun—or moonlight pale
They wandered in the August prime
   By Paint Creek's hill and dale.

    HILLSBORO, O.,|March 22, 1892.

THE OLD FARM HOUSE. (14)

STILL stands the house, a relic of the past;
  Still flows the stream, in curves around the
    farm;
And memories linger while years have past
  O'er forms of those who gave the place a charm.

'Twas years ago—at least to us it seems,
  When all this scene was radiant with delight,
When each and all in day or nightly dreams
  Thought home no fairer rose on earthly sight.

So far away that time and yet so near,
  When measured on infinity's long scroll;
No wonder recollection holds it dear,
  As when the farm house satisfied each soul.

Still flows the East Fork—gentle river,
  In curling outlines where glows the west,
And still the red sun with golden quiver
  Gleams o'er "the Bend" where all of yore were
    blest.

And once again the voices are repeating:
  The kindly words, that kindred find so dear,
When with affection every heart was beating
  In the Old Farm House so long ago!

"THE NEW YEAR COMES, MY LADY."

THE New Year comes my lady,
   At twelve the old year died,
Its burdens trailing after,
   Its worries cast aside—
In the drapery of silence,
   In the shadows of the pall
Its troubles—its distresses
   Are now beyond recall.

The morning dawns my lady,
   The tints in eastern sky
Are tokens of the coming day
   And hopes that must not die—
For the readings of the future
   In the horoscope are bright ;
Forebodings and repinings
   Have vanished with the night.

The sun is up my lady,
   There's glory in his face
As he fills the earth with beauty
   And crowns the hills with grace ;

Now as we make our orisons,
   Comes voice from Galilee :
" Let the dead bury the dead ;
   Do thou but follow me."

The work is waiting, lady,
   As antidote to harm ;
Charity with its blessing,
   Duties with their charm ;
For work makes life a pleasant thing,
   There is no time for woe ;
And bitter thoughts are banished
   Because we will it so.

THE OLD HAMMOCK. (15)

WHEN was first put up the hammock
    Children played upon the floor—
Curious, watching, artless children, ·
    Asking questions by the score.

Rolling, scrambling in the hammock,
    Filled with hope—they knew not sorrow
Fancy tinged with glorious promise
    Visions of each coming morrow.

    *   *   *   *   *

Swinging, swinging, idly swinging,
    Hopes have risen but to die,
Fancies faded with the morrow,
    As the days went fleeting by.

Grown the children—parents ageing,
    Since when at the evening tide,
Years ago, first swung the hammock, ·
    All the family side by side.

Swinging idly in the hammock,
    While upon the evening air
Tone of bells from steeple calling
    Worshipers to house of prayer.

Musing, dreaming, in the hammock
 Of the days that are no more,
When was first put up the hammock,
 Children watching from the floor.

Thinking, thinking, while is swinging
 Ancient hammock to and fro,
How the children, laughing, tumbled
 In its meshes long ago.

Swinging in the ancient hammock,
 Come again the vanished years,
And again are children playing,
 Innocent of cares or tears.

He from whom I bought the hammock
 As he passed it to my hand
Said : "With care 'twill last long after
 We are in the silent land."

Strange these words I yet remember
 Of the days that are no more,
Since my friend has crossed the river,
 Leaving me upon the shore.

All alone in swinging hammock,
 Hammock old and patched and torn,
Wondering which will last the longest,
 Man or hammock, aged and worn.

1894.

IN HOWE'S SEAT.

THIS is the spot—upon this knoll,
  Beneath which rushing waters flow,
Stood Henry Howe to sketch the scene
  Now more than fifty years ago.
In flush of youth he stood *just here*,
  Where beetling cliffs hang o'er the stream,
And by his pencil's magic art
  Pictured the landscape as a dream.

Howe heard from lips that now are mute
  The clust'ring legends centered here.
From living lips we heard the same
  Amid the haunts to us so dear,
Of Massie's camp and savage raids,
  Of captives bound and Indian trail,
Of Mussett's death and Huron chief
  And Etowah's pathetic tale.

The legends HOPE alone can tell,
  Of pioneers in days of yore,
More pleasure gave than all the tomes
  Of Greek or Roman classic lore.

The moments passed in charmed array
 'Till evening's sombre sunset glow.
When thinking of good Henry Howe,
 Reluctantly, we rose to go.

Thus we three left the wonderland,
 Where still the rushing waters flow,
Just as they did for Henry Howe,
 In times so many years ago.
Gorges and cliffs remain as then,
 Still lovely are the inter-vales,
And HOPE still lives—at twilight hour
 To tell the legendary tales.

1894.

BY WOODLAND PATHS.

YOU speak, my friend, of other lands,
    Of sights beyond the stormy seas,
Of wanderings in France and Spain,
    Of Alpine heights and Pyrenees ;
Of Paris with its boulevards,
    And Rome with stores of classic art,
Of turrets, spires and lordly halls,
    Of scenes in which *you* took a part.

You steamed, you say, down River Rhine,
    And saw its many ruins old—
And walked Cathedrals' fretted aisles,
    'Mid sculptured saints with crowns of gold.
Of London's crowded maze you tell,
    It's monuments and lofty dome,
And all *you* saw or heard abroad
    Surpasses what *we* have at home.

You fell in love with foreign ways,
    And quite forgot your native land,
While groping in the musty past
    With tourist guide book in your hand.

You now repeat the thread bare tales,
  Conned carefully from oral lore,
Repeated by the lying guides
  Who keep for *you* a stock in store.

Some others, too, have crossed the seas
  And wandered much on foreign shores,
They, *too*, have read the guide book lies
  About the sights *which turned out bores!*
Have sauntered, too, on boulevards,
  And threaded London's crowded maze,
While sculptures rare and paintings old
  Where subject to their curious gaze.

They did not yearn to change their lot,
  Or gush o'er everything at hand,
Because, before they crossed the seas
  Something they knew of native land,
They first had seen *our* wide domain,
  And knew it well from shore to shore,
Then when at last they crossed the seas
  They understood things, *may be*, more.

THE curtain of the years uplifts,
  And through the vistas wide
The camera of the mind portrays
  A rugged mountain side—
A winding path by aspen groves,
  A spring in sheltered nook,
A little chapel near the bridge
  Which spans a shallow brook—
A country road—a hostelry,
  A lawn with noble trees,
And children's artless voices borne
  Upon the evening breeze.
From the parlors, sound of music,
  And tramping in the hall,
On the porches happy faces,
  And a glamour over all.
There may be hearts uneasy
  And spirits sad and sore,
'Mid the shimmer of the dresses
  And the jeweled hands galore.
But still they do not show it,
  As fades the evening light,
And the German and the Lancers
  Fill up the pause of night.

The season fairly opened
  Is at its golden prime,
And gaiety and revel reigned
  That far-off summer time—
If ever came a weariness
  Then from the swelling tide
'Twas pleasanter to wander off
  And seek the mountain side.

II.

The August sun had sunk below
  The crown of western hill,
And from the hazel coverts near
  Came notes of whip-poor-will,
As down the path a fairy form
  Had reached the woody glade
Where a stranger tourist in the glen
  His wandering footsteps stayed.
She tripping came with bow in hand
  Clothed in Diana's grace,
And held the sense of stranger fast
  With haunting pretty face.
Her calm gray eyes and gentle speech
  Did not betoken wrath,
And soon they two, seemed like old friends
  Upon the mountain path.
There is poetry in motion,
  Companionship in voice,

And the pleasure of existence
   Is determined by the choice—
While the beauty of the summer
   Where nature rules alone
Is more lovely made when woman
   Gives it character and tone.

III.

Go see the springs in autumn
   When cruel winds have blown
The red and yellow emblems
   Of the forests bare and shorn—
And the moaning of the hemlocks
   Sounds like a wail of wrath
O'er the glories of the summer
   And the fairies of the path.
Then turn in retrospection
   To the far-off August time,
Which lingers still at even-tide
   With summer in its prime.
And never came a closing day
   When sun is sinking low
Without a thought of mountain strolls
   In days of long ago.
The little drama at the springs,
   Though on a *real* stage,
Is acted still in other spots
   And lives from age to age—

Though still to one may often come
  A radiant vision fair
Of dreamy days amid the hills
  When such good friends were there.
The last good-bye is spoken low,
  It brings remembered thrill
As camera catches fairy forms
  Upon the wooded hill.
While tone of voice and calm gray eye
  Now re-enact their part
Just as was wont, the mountain maid,
  When capturing a heart—
And the summer's idyl passing by
  Unreal as a play,
Where pageant kings and mimic queens
  Live out their little day,
Is but a dream, the actors gone
  No more to meet again,
And mountain path and storied spring
  In solitude remain—
In woodland depths where fairy forms
  Were tripping in their grace,
And where they stay'd the wanderer
  With haunting, pretty face.
The leaves are green in August time,
  And still from laurelled hill
Is heard at eve the saddened tone
  Of lonely whip-poor-will—

While still are men and women, too,
   Who follow nature's plan,—
Who make of life a pleasant thing
   And do the best they can—
For such as these, by sea or shore,
   By mountain path or glen,
Live memories of friendships formed
   In wanderings now and then.

HILLSBORO, O., January, 1894.

AT OLD SWEET SPRINGS, WEST VIRGINIA.

I AM back from a stroll in the valley
  Resting quietly in my chair,
While people are passing like phantoms
  And drowsiness hovers in air.
At "Old Sweet" sitting at leisure
  The tired limbs taking a rest,
While fancy may wander at pleasure
  Among old friends truest and best.
We walk through wide-reaching vistas
  So familiar does every spot seem
'Tis hard to distinguish the real
  From the shadowy lures of a dream.
And the summers come back while sleeping
  And gardens of memory rise,
While the years have staid on their journey
  And brightness glows in the eyes.
The friends of the past are still living,
  No sorrows have ever had birth
And together in Hills of Virginia
  We are walking the beautiful earth.
Thus dreaming away in the twilight
  All alone in the seat on the lawn
I talk with friends now departed
  Who have entered the land of the dawn.

Thus here in the Hills of Virginia
　　Where time stays the journeying years
We old friends rambled together,
　　'Ere life bore its guerdon of tears.

　　*　　　*　　　*　　　*　　　*　　　*

The Nun robed clouds were drifting
　　O'er the distant mountains gray
And the veil-of night was drooping
　　In the shadows of the day.
The cottage lights were gleaming
　　'Mid the foliage of the trees
And the murmurous sound of music
　　Was wafted on the breeze.
While the belles of Old Virginia
　　Were gathering in their pride,
The voices of " The Summer Girl "
　　Arose at eventide.
The lethargy of afternoon
　　Has sunk in Lethe's stream
And music summons tripping feet
　　To ball-room's radiant gleam.
We arouse to the call of the present
　　And past days trouble no more.
Let the past drift out to the ocean
　　And pick up the shells on the shore.
So we join in the nightly assemblage
　　Their faces with pleasure aglow

Among them we are not as strangers
    Or they would not welcome us so.
There is dignity, grace and good-feeling
    With its spell on the sense and the sight
And the eve at " Old Sweet " is resplendent
    With youth in its charm and its light.

August, 1894.

DRIFTING. (19)

I.

A DRIFT on the billowy ocean
    Amidst the crested waves,
Where the tempests blow from lands of snow,
  O'er Sea Kings' nameless graves :
    And the cold, cold stars their vigils keep
    As we drift and drift on trackless deep, ˙
Drift far on the stormy ocean,
  Amid phosphoric waves,
Where midnight gleams, in silver streams,
  From Naid's coral caves.

II.

The tremulous clouds are floating :
  The mist is gath'ring fast,
While the storm-fiend moans, in sullen tones,
  Around the shrouded mast,
    And the white ships over the distant main,
    Go sailing by in a phantom train,
Where tremulous clouds are floating
  Across the shining lea,
And moon hangs low, with yellow bow,
  As we drift on sparkling sea.

III.

There's glamour in the vision,
  Which sees in glad surprise
The mermaids fair, with glowing hair,
  From glist'ning waters rise.
    And lovers fond on the taffrail rest
    As they speak the words forever blest.
While the spell is on the ocean
  And the words are not in vain,
There are those who know that never below
  Will youth return again.

IV.

And the night shall wane in morning
  As we drift on the crested foam,
And day by day, shall the billows play
  O'er the giant Kraken's home.
    We see the fin of the hungry shark,
    Who prowls for prey where the depths are
      dark,
And the glow of early morning,
  As the waves each other chase,
Show the dolphin's dash in circling flash
  With sharks in eager race.

V.

The restless petrels hover
  Where sea-weed idly floats

Medusale drift, in ocean rift,
  And Nautilus' chambered boats.
    And the spell of the Lotus covers all
    With a dream of the buried sea-king's hall ;
Thus we drift from morn 'till ev'ning
  Amidst the crested waves,
And hear the moans, in wooing tones
  Of mermaids in their caves.

                    VI.

And the soul is wrap't in musing
  On the distant trees and hills
Where the wild birds sing on rust'ling wing,
  And flow the gurgling rills.
    And the haunted sea shall not beguile
    With its silver scales and mocking smile,
While the soul in fancy wanders,
  As we drift by night and day,
To the far off hills and gurgling rills
  Where the little children play.

  July, 1883.

PERE MARQUETTE. (20)

I.

THE Summer's breath is on the Island h eight
   The Great Lakes glitter in the August sun :
I see the sails of Commerce in the light
   And trailing lines of smoke in pall of dun.
But shadowy forms float dimly to the view ;
   I hear the wild Huron's rude refrain,
From Birch canoes with dusty phantom crew
   The convoy of a funeral train.

II.

There, where the pine a length'ning shadow throws,
   Reflecting from the wave each spear and leaf,
Behold an humble, hallowed altar glows,
   And the dark Ottawa, with his wail of grief.
I hear the wierd chanting sad and slow,
   And see as in a dream the buried years,
The waxen candles brightly burn, and lo
   The fevered world has vanished with its cares.

III.

The loving Priest and Father early lost
　Arises with a luster from the tomb ;
His brow is white with Heaven's pearly frost,
　And Pere Marquette appears in fadeless bloom.
Here are no paths of trade, or scenes of mirth,
　The throbbing soul is turned to sky above ;
This humble priest shall give your thoughts new
　　birth
　Whose life was holy faith, and peace, and love.

IV.

Soon from this shore the marble shaft shall rise,
　Where rests the Martyr's consecrated dust,
A beacon to the wand'ring tourist's eyes,
　A pledge of all that's perfect, true and just.
The kings of trade lie in forgotten graves,
　Who changed to bloody scenes this land of peace,
But Marquette's fame shall hallow all these waves
' Till Time itself shall in oblivion cease.

　　August 14, 1884.

YOU AND I.

IN crimson hills where glows the evening sun,
  Upon the leafy summits high,
And maples quiver in their robes of dun,
  We wander dreaming, *you and I.*
We see the dropping chestnuts fall at close of day,
  And the red-garbed sumach bar our devious
      way.—
The giant oaks which skirt the mountains old,
  The dogwoods on the valley side,
The tangled thickets with their crowns of gold,
  And water gurgling at eve'ning tide.
October music fills the wood and sky,
Deep in the hills where wander *you and I.*

II.

We see on hoary rocks the lines of light
  'Mid fitful shadows grim and wild,
With rippling streamlets flashing to the sight
  And gently whisp'ring like a child.—
We sit beside the bubbling spring and beech,
  Far from the world, yet world within our reach,
And ponder long 'mid crimson hills
  Where nature to all good gives birth,

In tree and flower and flowing rills
   And sounds of joy and peace and mirth.
So falls the night—so calm the sky,
And calm our souls—both *you and I.*

  October 11th, 1885.

CHESTER ON THE DEE.

A REMINISCENCE.

W E came from freedom's sacred land,
    Across the western sea,
To ramble through old Chester town
    Upon the River Dee.
The summer sun had risen fair,
    The lark sang loud in glee,
What time we strolled in Chester town,
    In Chester on the Dee.

The gentle waters softly flow,
    To mingle with the tide,
And green the shining holly fringe
    Begirts the river side.
The ivy climbs the Roman wall,
    Clings to the turret high,
Creeps o'er Saint Werburgh's Abbey dome,
    Outlined upon the sky.

We tread the vast cathedral aisles,
    And gaze in silent awe,
On spots where Cæsar's eagles flew
    Ere Saxons gave the law.

Where Norman crushed the beaten Celt ;
  With heavy burdens sore,
And Roundhead smote gay Cavalier,
  On field of Rowton Moor.

We see the smiling landscape spread,
  Where art and nature vie,
With park, and church and castle crown'd
  To charm the tourists' eye.
We stand upon the time worn bridge,
  And wonder can it be,
That we are here in Chester town,
  In Chester on the Dee ?

We hear the bells in Abbey spire
  Chime at the close of day,
And we must turn from Chester town
  Upon our wandering way.
The shepherds led the distant flocks,
  From marshes by the sea,
And fishers draw their evening nets
  In waters of the Dee.

And never more our eyes may rest
  Upon the glowing lea,
Our feet no more shall walk the streets
  Of Chester on the Dee,

For low has sank the summer sun
   On all the fairy scene,
We pluck the glist'ning holly leaves
   And clust'ring ivy green.

The Christmas chimes from Abbey dome,
   Sound o'er the Roman wall,
The Shepherd good, proclaimeth peace,
   On earth good will to all.
The fisher for the souls of men,
   The Man of Galilee,
Takes thought for each, while Christmas bells
   Chime on the River Dee.

The Book of Books is opened wide,
   To tell the story old
Of Him who for us all hath died.
   The shepherd of the fold.
While 'neath the lamplight clust'ring hangs,
   A mem'ry of the sea,
The Christmas holly, ivy green,
   From Chester on the Dee.

December, 1884.

CHATTANOOGA.

O SLEEPER, rise ! the dawn is here ;
 This is historic ground.
Shall tourists sleep, where legions fought,
 And squadrons camped around,
And where this city sits in pride,
 Immortal fame was found ?

Behold the glint of purple morn,
 Fades slowly into dun,
And violet hues in Eastern skies,
 Show golden in the sun—
And the crashing of the hemlocks
 Shows deadly work begun !

For time turns back a score of years,
 To another Autumn day,
When Hooker led his warrior's charge,
 In battle's fierce array,
Through thunder clouds to mountain crest
 Up, up, the shell-torn way !

Now creeping through the rifts of mist
   The lines of Blue appear—
The cannon's dull and heavy roar
   And scream of shells we hear,
While stern the rugged mountain frowns
   So far and yet so near!

Is this the gleam of bayonets
   Upon the cloudy sea?
What are those forms in misty gray
   Which o'er the chasms flee?
Is not that flag on Lookout point,
   The banner of the free?

Come turn the glass, on yonder cleft,
   Beside the awful peak,
Where heroes rush 'mid hurling shot—
   Honor in death to seek,
And where each spot these soldiers fell
   Their glory yet doth speak.

And every rock and shrub and tree,
   On mountain's war-scarred brow,
Each rusted shell, or broken gun
   Turned up by Southern plow
A story tells of those who fell
   To make us freemen now!

Oh Pilgrims of another age,
   Unscatched by war's dread quiver?
O'er Chickamauga's blood-stained plain,
   O'er Mission Hill and river,
And sentinel Lookout's regal crown
   The stars shall watch forever.

On STANTON HOUSE PORCH. November, 1885.

TRILOGY.

I.

Certum pete finem.—(THE LAW STUDENT.)

THERE never lived a man and never will,
    Who could not keep hotel or run a mill
Or think so, in his blind conceit and try
'Till taught by sad experience by and by.
The Lawyer like the Artisan is made
By careful study, in his youth displayed :
No "*ad-captandum*" talent—but set rules
To learn when, and how, to handle tools.
"*Aim at a certain end,*" and seek the goal
With the set purpose of your heart and soul.
Don't wander off amid delusion's rays,
While plodding comrades follow beaten ways.
Make Law your text—avoid alluring verse,
For the true student, nothing can be worse
Against the Muse, the Law is up in arms,
With knitted brow at mention of her charms.
Entrance is closed on Law's majestic heights,
To winged Pe-ga-sus in his dreamy flights.
Then dally not 'mid perfumed blossoms sweet,
Which with enchantment all your senses greet.

Avoid, yon muse, the mountain, lake or sea,
To scribble sonnets, pleasant though it be,
Since in *this* field, the prizes to be gained
Will turn to ashes if at last attained.
In Law, and Law alone, your future lies,
And not in Siren Poesy's luring eyes
On all *belles lettres* you must scowling frown,
Or abandon hope of the ermined gown.

II.

Inter Nos.—(THE YOUNG LAWYER.)

No footsteps backward—"the die is cast"
The Rubicon of Doubt is safely passed.
Like Cortez sailing o'er the Spanish main,
Who burned his ships on reaching Aztic plain,
You venture through a tangled maze to meet
Your unknown foes, and cut off all retreat
Within the confines of our Storied Bar
"Where Fame's proud Temple gleams afar"
You stand elate upon the shores of youth
The champion armoured in the cause of truth.
In learnèd Courts, with Justice painted blind,
The Law to state, and righteous judgment find.
The field is ample for the gleaners still,
As seats are vacant, others come to fill.
Themis your mistress, holds here the honor'd place,
Allows no other to obscure her grace.

Enter the lists to combat for *the* right
One *vade mecum* constant keep in sight,
"Though you and comrades often disagree,
Between ourselves—always make sure
             You'r Fee."

III.

Sic eunt fata hominum.—(THE OLD LAWYER.

The time *will* come—it may be years or days
You must forego the Forum's thorny ways,
Leave off your Briefs, nor give a single thought
To all the hot forensic battles fought.
Abandon all the occult webs of Law,
Those mystic arts to keep mankind in awe.
No more the anxious hours of former years,
While 'waiting verdicts with your boding fears,
When all the trophies of a proud career,
You cast aside and can not shed a tear
When Fate shall draw you from the Bar apart,
With only memories lingering in the heart.
With vanished Past as *mirage* of the plain
No more to cause you either joy or pain,
'Though there are scenes you never can forget
And much perhaps in later years regret.
To Judges, Juries and our Brethren true
To each and all Time brings a last adieu !
"Thus go the fates of men " in peace or war,
Thus Time will deal with members of the Bar."

AT FORT DOUGLAS, UTAH, OCTOBER, 1894.

WE gaze upon the distant lake
   (As fires the evening gun)
With the gleam upon Oquirrah
   From the sinking autumn sun.
The white gulls rise where shadows creep,
   O'er islands purple hue
And silver streams are flowing o'er
   The waters green and blue.

What colors in the western sky
   The artist's tints to shame,
With orange, violet, ruby, gold,
   The Heaven's all aflame!
How clear and pure the atmosphere
   How soft the evening breeze
How near the distant city seems
   In garniture of trees!

Well it shall be for those brave souls
   Whose steps were not in vain,
Who planted Eden's empire firm
   Upon a desert plain,

Where sand and sage and silence reigned
   In canyon, hill and dell,
The gardens bloom—and waters run
   Like sound of tinkling bell.

The snow-clad Wasatch towers above
   The red-rocked fort below,
And from the canyon crystal streams
   In music rippling flow,
The mountains of the ages old,
   Behold our banner fly,
The starry emblem of our hope
   For freedom 'neath the sky.

The mountains guard the circled plains,
   The fort, the city fair,
And while the giant hills shall stand
   Our flag shall float in air,
The flag which borne through rugged ways
   By men devoid of fear,
Shall cover with its sheltering folds
   The pilgrims settled here.

NOTES.

(1) These little Alpine flowers grow on all the high Colorado summits, and there are said to be other varieties unknown in the Alps. It is a strange sight to see these little flowers peeping up from the snow amid everlasting desolation. There are also four varieties of the cactus, which grow at lofty altitudes and are impervious to the coldest weather.

(2) Who has not seen the picture of one solitary figure standing on the rocks of St. Helena, with folded arms and looking out on the limitless sea?

(3) Written on the Ocean, in 1883, while the author was bound for Europe.

(4) Recalling the first visit of the author to Manitou in 1886.

(5) *Sangre de Cristo* is the poetic and religious name given by the Spaniards, meaning "The Blood of Christ"—the *Fontaine que Bouille*, French for boiling water. *Pueblo*, means people, or a town of vanquished Indians.

(6) From Muntz hill, overlooking the highway leading from Hillsboro to Belfast.

(7) The colors of the Calverts were black and orange. The Oriole, which has the same markings, was hence called "The Baltimore Oriole." The English sparrow has driven the beautiful Fire-bird away from most localities.

(8) Written at the Glen House, White Mountains, for Miss Stella Beeson, July, 1892. The next morning our tourist party left for the seashore. The references are to "Emerald Pool" and the river near Glen House.

(9) Mr. F. W. Armstrong was educated in Paris, and passed daily through the *Jardin de Luxembourg* to school in the Latin Quartier, to which allusion is made in the poem.

(10) Written in Queenston harbor, August 27, 1883, for some emigrants going to America.

(11) Stanzas for music. Liverpool, England, July 7, 1883.

(12) From Eglise Madeleine, to Colonne de Juliet, erected on spot where the Bastile stood. This is the oldest of the Paris Boulevards.

(13) Written for the Columbus Camera Club.

(14) This poem was dedicated to the author's aunt of Dayton, Ohio, and refers to a well-known mansion in the Elk Lick Valley, near Bantam. It bears date, June, 1892.

(15) The hammock was purchased from Dr. H. S. Fullerton, since deceased.

(16) Henry W. Hope, referred to, is an old and intelligent resident of Ohio's Wonderland, and is an estimable citizen who has done much for the locality, and is held in high regard by all who know him.

(17) Adams Co., Ohio, Mineral Springs.

(18) Written on the Ocean in July, 1883, while drifting on steamer Belgravia in the Gulf Stream, owing to her machinery being disabled.

(19) See Parkman's sketch of burial of Marquette by the Indians. A monument to his memory has been erected at Point St. Ignace.

(20) An impromptu in the Brush Creek Hills, October 11, 1885.